IMAGINE!
THOUGHT-PROVOKING POETRY

CREATIVE VOICES

Edited By Wendy Laws

First published in Great Britain in 2021 by:

YoungWriters®
Est. 1991

Young Writers
Remus House
Coltsfoot Drive
Peterborough
PE2 9BF
Telephone: 01733 890066
Website: www.youngwriters.co.uk

All Rights Reserved
Book Design by Ashley Janson
© Copyright Contributors 2021
Softback ISBN 978-1-80015-294-6

Printed and bound in the UK by BookPrintingUK
Website: www.bookprintinguk.com
YB0467AZ

FOREWORD

Since 1991, here at Young Writers we have celebrated the awesome power of creative writing, especially in young adults, where it can serve as a vital method of expressing their emotions and views about the world around them. In every poem we see the effort and thought that each pupil published in this book has put into their work and by creating this anthology we hope to encourage them further with the ultimate goal of sparking a life-long love of writing.

Our latest competition for secondary school students, Imagine, challenged young writers to delve into their imaginations to conjure up alternative worlds where anything is possible. We provided a range of speculative questions to inspire them from 'what if kids ruled the world?' to 'what if everyone was equal?' or they were free to use their own ideas. The result is this creative collection of poetry that imagines endless possibilities and explores the consequences both good and bad.

We encourage young writers to express themselves and address subjects that matter to them, which sometimes means writing about sensitive or contentious topics. If you have been affected by any issues raised in this book, details on where to find help can be found at www.youngwriters.co.uk/info/other/contact-lines

CONTENTS

All Saints Catholic College, Dukinfield

Chloe Veale (12)	1
Jessica Pearce (12)	2
Molly Moores (12)	3
Mahmood Asjad (12)	4
Emily Pomfret (12)	5
Hamza Malik (13)	6
Leighton Hatton (13)	7
Holly Tickle (12)	8
Isabelle Texeira (13)	9
Erin Hodgson (12)	10
Jessica Hayes (12)	11
Eva Robison (13)	12
Davie Joyce (13)	13
Kimberley Kennedy (12)	14
Scarlett Henniker (12)	15
Charlotte Johnson (13)	16
Ruby Thornes (12)	17
Libby Taylor (12)	18
Daragh Mulcahy (12)	19
Abigail Pritchard (13)	20
Daisy Spedding (13)	21
Gabriel Ordon (12)	22
Jack Thornes (12)	23
Grace Holian (12)	24
Joanne Esiri (12)	25

Bentley Wood High School, Stanmore

Sahida Safi (11)	26
Asiyah Datoo (11)	28
Saaliha Kanani (12)	29
Nkiah Blake (15)	30

Sophia Karger (12)	31
Sarah Muraj (13)	32
Aneya Shah (11)	33
Iklas Haashi (11)	34
Jaimisha Patel (12)	35

Cansfield High School, Ashton-in-Makerfield

Ava Mae Holland (11)	36
Megan Pearce (11)	38
Katie Naylor (11)	39
Ben Sudworth (12)	40
Max Woosey (11)	41
Jake Pimblett (12)	42
Wojciech Pozniak (12)	43
Grace Cannon (12)	44
Lottie Walsh (12)	45
Faye Lawson (11)	46
Harry Paterson (12)	47
Theo Leyland (12)	48
Katie Jones (12)	49
Jack Mannion (11)	50
Lilly-Mae Robson (12)	51
Mia Blackwood (11)	52
Poppy Goulding (11)	53
Emma Pimblett (11)	54
Abbie Jones (12)	55
Daylan Sleigh-Geary (12)	56
Emily Pollitt (11)	57
Oliver Hodge (11)	58
Alesha Parr (11)	59
Esmé Skinner (12)	60
Summer Bell (11)	61
Isabelle Nisbet (11)	62
Leo Pimblett (11)	63

Oldbury Wells School, Bridgnorth

Camren Farrington-Hyrons (11)	64
Dylan Hill (12)	66
Benjamin Jordan (12)	67
Anna Cole (13)	68
Kimberley Kendall (12)	69
Nyima Winters (12)	70
Lydia Walker (12)	71

Ormiston Horizon Academy, Tunstall

Haajarah Tahir (12)	72
Gracie Harris (13)	73
Finley Sawyer (12)	74
Charlotte Plant (11)	75
Lexi Ashmall (13)	76
Jack Vickers (11)	77
Henry Hughes (11)	78
Ava Harvey-Gibson (12)	79
Josh Duncan (12)	80
Delilah May Brough (12)	81
Aimeé-Grace Shaw (13)	82
Esme West (11)	83
Millie Rafferty (12)	84
Ruby-Mai Mountford (12)	85
Millie Elson (13)	86
Brian Boulton (12)	87
Tom Smith (13)	88
Elise Robinson (13)	89
Vanessa Popko (11)	90
Evan Kinsey (12)	91
Megan Nixon (14)	92
Grace Leigh (12)	93
Ryan Colclough (13)	94
Patrick Chapinski (13)	95
Jensen Grocott (13)	96
Ellie-Mae Condliffe (12)	97
Lillie Jones (12)	98
Aleksandra Grosiak (12)	99
Amber Louise Pateman (13)	100
Evan Jones (12)	101
Emily Jane Harris (13)	102
Emma Davis (13)	103
Lexie Jones (12)	104
Brendan Dawson (13)	105
Jack Hardy (13)	106
Lucy Batho (13)	107
Jay Balmer (14)	108
Craig Jones (13)	109
Abbie Golinski (12)	110
Amelie Barlow (13)	111
AJ Ball (13)	112
Connor Flesher (12)	113
Isabelle Burrows (11)	114
Tom Duffy (14)	115
Oscar Robinson (12)	116
Alyssa Bolderson (12)	117
Ben Luis Oliver (13)	118
Lottie Hancock (11)	119
Jacob Fryer (11)	120
Eliza Glenn (12)	121
Eleanor Green (13)	122
Dale Jenkins-Ferriday (13)	123
Ella Potts (13)	124
Lily Talbot (12)	125
Daniel Moran (13)	126
Lola Tyler (11)	127
Sharna Laud (11)	128
Joseph Moorse (13)	129
Joel Sims (13)	130
Katie Guy (13)	131
Reuben Dapaah Bonsu	132

St Mark's West Essex Catholic School, Harlow

Sienna Smith (11)	133
Lucja Ostrowska (11)	134
Willow Druce (11)	135
Isabel Nye (11)	136
Evie Wills (11)	137
Karson Dhakal (14)	138
Naglis Arlauskas (11)	139
Christina Lacey (12)	140
Jenna Bennett (11)	141
Kajus Skauronas (11)	142

THE POEMS

Imagine - Creative Voices

Trapped In Mineland

T he world is filled with blocks and too many people
R andomly the world was being mined with axes
A land in a computer screen
P eople believing in random things
P eople loved it and some hated it
E very person had a bad opinion but some had a good opinion
D ullness, lightness, sunny, freezing, nobody could tell.

I t was weird, creepy, isolated in my opinion
N o one knew about it except the people who were there

M e and myself, it was unusually strange but fun
I magine if everyone knew about us
N obody told anyone at all, no one knew
E veryone was so secretive about it
L earning wasn't an option, you had to work all day
A nd the job of mining everything may seem easy but it's not
N ew buildings vanished without fail
D igging was the only thing I was allowed to do.

Chloe Veale (12)
All Saints Catholic College, Dukinfield

Imagine

Imagine if you started suffering from mental health in the blink of an eye.
Imagine if no one believed you as you kept saying you're fine.
Imagine being made fun of because others thought you were an attention seeker.
Imagine constantly being overwhelmed about the smallest of things.
Imagine if you ended up having to lie to people to keep them happy.
Imagine not being able to tell anyone about it.
Imagine if this happened to you.
This is what not being able to take off your mask can feel like.
Imagine if you started believing every insult and lie.
Imagine you did not believe any compliment.
Many people suffer from this,
Try asking that one friend who is always smiling,
Are they actually okay? And not just saying they are.
Don't judge others, you don't know if something is happening to them
Or what has happened to make them like they are.

Jessica Pearce (12)
All Saints Catholic College, Dukinfield

Imagine If You Had One Wish

Imagine if you had one wish,
You could wish for the world to be peaceful
Or that you ruled the world
Or maybe you could become invisible.
There is so much you could wish for.
You only have one wish,
What will you do...?

There is so much for you to wish for
But don't think it out loud or it won't come true.
Think long and hard that's what you must do.

Listen to your heart.
I don't think you should get that,
It could fall apart.
Come on now think long and hard.

Imagine if you had one wish,
You could wish for more but don't be selfish.
I know you will decide in just a bit of time,
But remember don't waste it, just think very hard.
I'm going now,
I'll be back in a short amount of time,
But for now,
Just imagine if you had one wish...

Molly Moores (12)
All Saints Catholic College, Dukinfield

Imagine You Found Out You're In A Game

G oing in a game is a dream for everyone
R unning, driving or doing stunts
A s I walked down the street I saw people breaking rules
N ot knowing I was in a game, I was afraid
D id I or did I not find out I was in a game?

T o be rich was a dream, robbing banks like it was nothing
H unting for criminals like it was nothing
E rasing my tasks every time I did one
F or goodness' sake I got shot but I had health
T urning my back to the wall as I got shot.

A round me were gangsters surrounding me
U nderstanding how they move so I could escape
T o myself I thought I was gonna die
O ver the walls as I climbed them, got in the car and drove as fast as I could.

Mahmood Asjad (12)
All Saints Catholic College, Dukinfield

Imagine; My Reality

Imagine a wall
blocking out light,
watching civilisation rise and fall.
Imagine living your whole life
dreaming of an outside,
not knowing of its strife.
Imagine getting to the age of ten
and never seeing the sea,
not knowing if ever, not when.
Imagine climbing a tall oak tree
that grows next to the wall,
just a peek, just a see.
Imagine looking expecting gold,
rivers of chocolate, proud mountains stood tall,
but being confronted by nothing of which you were told.
Imagine seeing nothing but soot
blocking the sky, choking the world,
making you shiver from head to foot.
Imagine it's your reality
because it's mine,
isolated, watching the time,
awaiting the world outside's fatality.

Emily Pomfret (12)
All Saints Catholic College, Dukinfield

Imagine If Dreams Were Real

Imagine if dreams were real,
All the people in the world will be finally free.
Flying around, all colourful,
Cars in the beautiful sky.
There will not be people who have bad lives.
The poor will finally be rich.
The poor in heart will be happy.
Imagine the vibrant colours,
Kids outside having the time of their lives,
All bad in the world will be gone,
Everything will be possible...
Flying cars,
Superpowers,
A robot society.
Imagine having all the knowledge in the world,
You would know the secrets to life
And what is out there that we cannot explore.
We would be able to fly around in space,
Meet aliens and visit new planets
And see what's out there.

Hamza Malik (13)
All Saints Catholic College, Dukinfield

If Ninjago Was Real

If Lego Ninjago was a reality
There would be six ninjas roaming the streets.
Spinjitzu masters and elemental pros.
Fire, water, ice and lightning,
Earth and energy and a sensei master.
A four-armed beast will take over
And fight his son Lloyd Montgomery Garmadon
But he is not the worst of all,
There will be an evil spirit who is more powerful than ever,
He goes by the name of Overlord.

There are many more villains,
Too many to be found,
But the ninjas will take care,
Riding on dragons, using elemental weapons.
Of all these fools, sacrifices, fallouts, family reunions,
That is what will happen in Ninjago was real,
A terrifying world made out of Lego.

Leighton Hatton (13)
All Saints Catholic College, Dukinfield

Imagine If I Could Change The Past

Imagine if I could change the past,
Erasing the things I ever said that would hurt someone,
Being proud about the things I did well.
Changing my mind from when I couldn've had fun but said no.
Saying my thoughts instead of holding them in.
Being happy instead of worrying about what others think of me.
Reminisce on the days when I was excited.
Take away the times I took anger out on everyone else
And just keep it all to myself.
Saying something to my friends I know I didn't mean,
To make it something that'll make them feel good about themselves,
Even just a smile or make them feel proud.
Wouldn't that just feel great?
Imagine if I could change the past.

Holly Tickle (12)
All Saints Catholic College, Dukinfield

Year 3030

Imagine it's the year 3030, you're the last one,
Nothing left, not even a single animal.
I live off leaves, fish, grass and rainwater as my drink.
Imagine if there is nothing.
No doctors. No farmers. No family. No friends. No anything.
Except me. Why me?
Why was I chosen to live on after all humanity? Why?
As I walk down the treacherous street,
Wondering if there is someone out there,
I begin the trip across this isolated world.
After many years of being alone -
I will finally be able to answer the question that I ask myself every day,
Is there someone out there?
I might never know. But I will never give up.
I am hopeful.
Well, I think I am.

Isabelle Texeira (13)
All Saints Catholic College, Dukinfield

Everything Was Normal

Imagine if everything was normal,
Imagine if there was no hate to the world,
No terrorism, no racism, no knife crime.
Imagine if everything was normal.

Imagine if everything was normal,
There would be no pandemic, no Covid-19,
No children going to school with mates,
No parents worrying about their jobs.
Imagine if everything was normal.

Imagine if everything was normal,
No homeless children or parents on the streets,
No refugees or endangered animals,
No people fleeing from their homes because of war.
Imagine if everything was normal.

Imagine it all, everyone would be happy,
Imagine, just imagine.

Erin Hodgson (12)
All Saints Catholic College, Dukinfield

Imagine If You Were Dead

Imagine if you were dead
Going through your memories, everything you'd said.
See your loved ones again,
Or had they gone insane?

Seeing everything on Earth,
Every death, every birth.
See the afterlife,
What would you find?
Would you mind?

How would your family react?
Would you go back?

Heaven, hell or purgatory?
Seems just like a scary story.
Alive or dead, is it all the same?
Do you still go through the pain?
Would you be scared or calm?

Did death do you any harm?
Did you lose a leg or an arm?
Who knows but me,
I'm the only one that can see...

Jessica Hayes (12)
All Saints Catholic College, Dukinfield

Death

Imagine if you had the option to die.
Imagine being able to say to someone I am going to die.
Imagine being in pain and being able to stop it.
Imagine the thought of being able to put an end to life.
Imagine if you left everyone behind.
Imagine if you could control your life.
Imagine if you could go and speak to your family members.
Imagine if you could come back from heaven and tell people what it is like.
Imagine being able to stop all of your life.
Imagine lighting a candle and it burning out.
Imagine the light disappearing.
Imagine once that light has disappeared
You are no more.

Eva Robison (13)
All Saints Catholic College, Dukinfield

The Afterlife

Imagine when you died,
Everything went black
And you were losing your grasp of hope
And were falling to your doom.
But your dejected mood will change.
You smell the grass
And the fresh air.

Imagine if the world was peaceful
And you could hear the birds singing.
Everything looks like it has been resumed.
The fresh new trees stood proud of its appearance,
You could do anything in this majestic green land.

Imagine if you were calm
And pondering on a bench,
While you enjoy your everlasting life.
Is this heaven?
Yes.

Davie Joyce (13)
All Saints Catholic College, Dukinfield

A Ghost Town

Imagine if you were the last person alive,
Just you.
I had a question in my mind,
Why me?
Everything, everyone and you chased me.
As I walked down empty, silent streets,
A cool fresh breeze blew down on my face.
Silent air whistled through my head.
Everything was gone, no animals, no people and no family,
Everything was a ghost town.
I had now forgotten what life was.
Walking, talking, eating was different.
If I had a rewind button,
I would change everything back to normal.
I was a ghost.
Life was different.
Just imagine.

Kimberley Kennedy (12)
All Saints Catholic College, Dukinfield

Imagine If Time Froze

Imagine if time froze,
Imagine how cool that would be,
Imagine how quiet it would be,
Imagine having no one to bother you,
Imagine not hearing a sound,
Imagine no one walking or talking,
Imagine if the world was at peace.

Imagine if you were stuck like this forever,
Imagine how miserable that would be,
Imagine how lonely you would be,
Imagine if you had no one to talk to,
Imagine how sad that would be,
Imagine seeing your loved ones stuck, never being able to talk to them again,
Imagine how cool and miserable that would be!

Scarlett Henniker (12)
All Saints Catholic College, Dukinfield

Imagine

Imagine if the world was a lie,
If it was a computer system
Which hooked into our brains
And just waited for us to die.

A torture device used
By evil spies,
While we were 'living our lives',
They would hack our bodies and use us as slaves.

They say we only use
10% of our brain,
But what if that's not what we use,
But what is accessible?

Imagine a control panel
Where all our memories are stored
And the thing in charge, there stroking its cat,
Can you imagine that?

Charlotte Johnson (13)
All Saints Catholic College, Dukinfield

Sometimes I Imagine

Sometimes I imagine a perfect family
When in reality my family is in rage,
Uprooted from the ground.

Sometimes I imagine a shiny red brick house
When in reality my house is dark, dirty and deformed.

Sometimes I imagine having a happy childhood,
When in reality I feel like I raised myself.

Sometimes I imagine having two loving parents,
When in reality I have a constant headache.

I always imagine being the perfect child
When in reality I'm just a mistake and a disappointment.

Ruby Thornes (12)
All Saints Catholic College, Dukinfield

Imagine If You Were Invisible

Imagine if you were invisible,
You could sneak up on people
Without them knowing.
You could save the day
And save people from dropping a tray,
Without them knowing.

In one way
You could be evil,
Cause trouble
And stop a child from blowing a bubble.
You could hold so much power,
You could ruin a whole city,
That would be a pity.
Rob banks,
Be rich,
You could throw someone in a ditch.

But at the end of the day,
Imagine if you were invisible!

Libby Taylor (12)
All Saints Catholic College, Dukinfield

Imagine

Imagine being able to breathe underwater
and see all the tropical fish
but what if a shark passes by
I don't want to be on his dish!

Imagine being able to fly
I would touch the sky.
I know for certain that if I fell I wouldn't die,
I would rest on the clouds warm in a fleece
and I would rest in peace.

Imagine being as fast as The Flash,
if someone chased me I would dash.
No one would catch me
and it would be fun
running under the warm, bright sun.

Daragh Mulcahy (12)
All Saints Catholic College, Dukinfield

Imagine If The Apocalypse Happened

If I was the only one left,
I would go insane,
My mental state put to the test.

Skyscrapers dissolved to thin air,
Mankind's hard work
Unable to be repaired.

I live in a town,
All alone,
Not another soul, not another sound.

On a daily hunt for food and more,
I stumbled into a wall
That I had never seen before.

Made of scraps of metal and brick,
Perhaps I am not alone,
I knocked on the wall with a stick.

Abigail Pritchard (13)
All Saints Catholic College, Dukinfield

Gone

Imagine if adults had vanished
All those above eighteen
Are now gone.
Imagine all the teenagers
Had turned the world into a warzone.
They formed groups and terrorised the outcasts.
Imagine if it was a purge,
Maybe the government had done this
Just to make us believe in aliens.
Maybe they'll turn the adults back,
Back to their normal selves,
Back to when they weren't dead.

Daisy Spedding (13)
All Saints Catholic College, Dukinfield

Into The Dark

Imagine falling endlesssly,
In the deep ocean,
Being able to see every creature,
Swimming down to the void below,
Stranger creatures the lower I go,
I look up, see a spark of light,
But still I fall endlessly into the night.
How long until I reach the bottom?
A day, a week,
Or even a year.
I dare not think
As I sink.

Gabriel Ordon (12)
All Saints Catholic College, Dukinfield

Imagine If You Could Travel To The Future

Imagine if you could travel to the future,
What would you see?
Robots, space ships, you could see it all,
You could see new discoveries,
You could see new world problems,
You could be the only one.

You could see the whole world rearrange right in front of your eyes.
You would be the only one on Earth to see this dramatic change.

Jack Thornes (12)
All Saints Catholic College, Dukinfield

Imagine If...

Imagine if you won the lottery,
What would you buy?
Gold and silver, copper too,
What would you do?

Would you buy happiness?
Would you buy health?
Would you spend it all on yourself?

Would you share it with your family?
Your friends too.
All the things you could buy,
What would you do?

Grace Holian (12)
All Saints Catholic College, Dukinfield

Alone

A nxiously, searching around
L ooking panicked because you can't hear a sound
O nly when you scream aloud
N obody is anywhere to be found
E veryone is gone, leaving their stuff on the ground.

Joanne Esiri (12)
All Saints Catholic College, Dukinfield

Imagine If They Know...

Heart pounding in my chest,
I look at the people around me.
Imagine - imagine if they know.
The horrifying truth shouldn't be known.

I run - run away.
I look at the man in front of me.
Imagine - imagine if he knows.
I hear my breath rattle in my chest.

I run - run as fast as I can.
My blood pounds in my ears.
I try to escape my threatening thoughts
But somehow, they find me.

I run - to a place I've never been to before.
A woman is walking on the other side of the road.
Imagine - imagine if she knows.
Run - I tell myself - run.

My legs ache, my head aches, but I still don't stop.
They can't know, I tell myself, they can't.
No one can - except for her.
But she isn't here, she can't be.

But as I start to walk away,
I see her emerge out of thin air.
She knows - I tell myself - she knows.

I scream a deafening scream.
It's over - she knows.

Sahida Safi (11)
Bentley Wood High School, Stanmore

Eyes Of Control

Taking control with just one stare,
While others sit back and snare,
All under my control,
Just watch out, stay on patrol.

Swirling round and round,
Look into my eyes but not around,
They say hypnotism isn't real,
But trust me it isn't that surreal.

All power will belong to me!
All shall bow down to me!
And only me!

The world you imagine,
A world from Aladdin,
Dreams shall come true,
For me and for you.

But watch out at night,
Be shielded by a knight,
For then you shall regret,
When I come round darkness burning from my silhouette.

Hop onto my side
And you shall leave undenied,
Your wishes my command,
If only I could rule the land.

Asiyah Datoo (11)
Bentley Wood High School, Stanmore

Colours

Colours, the bright luminous creation,
Surrounding everything from head to toe.
All the colours in the rainbow,
Everything has colour just you don't know.

Red, bright luscious red,
The cut on your finger or the heart in your chest,
Or the anger of someone taking what you love best,
Or the invisible devil, that cruel pest.

Green, bright fresh green,
The rainforest in Brazil or the grass that I step on,
Or the sin of jealousy or the vomit of your son,
Or the thought of losing your little hun.

Blue, bright clear blue,
The waves of the sea or the sadness of your eye,
Or the clear water that we drink or the whisper of a lie,
See, everything has a colour, even you and me but why...?

Saaliha Kanani (12)
Bentley Wood High School, Stanmore

Black Lives Matter

I stand and watch people I know be manipulated and led away
Leaving children alone and taking loved ones away
Families torn apart from a recurring sin
Oh there's so much, where do I begin?
And all of this because of the colour of my skin
Shouldn't my culture be a sacred thing?
That's why I cannot lay in wait, for the police to lay things straight
I must make a stand or will bear this fate
Imagine a world where we can be free
Walk into a store without people staring at me
Freedom is what we should be fighting for
Take this message and fight some more
I wish for the day where my sisters and brothers are free
What will be of the future? We soon shall see...

Nkiah Blake (15)
Bentley Wood High School, Stanmore

Reality Isn't Imagination

Why is the world a lie?
Why can't you reach for the clouds and touch the sky?
Sometimes you close your eyes and fall from a tree,
Then wake up realising it was a dream.
Take a leap of faith to see where you land,
Over a bridge or into the sand.

Reality isn't imagination,
It's like that all over the nation,
Not even that - the entire world,
inventing new words like maktuba or maliburld
Would only ever be in your head.
Like my dad said,
"Good job, lots of money,
In this world you don't need to be happy."

Sophia Karger (12)
Bentley Wood High School, Stanmore

Who Is My Mum?

Who is my mum? Who is my mum?
She is taken for granted say some,
But I don't think that,
She is the best person to chat,
She is closest to my heart,
But how did this connection start?
Eight months you carried me in your womb,
It felt as cosy as a room,
It must have caused a lot of painl
Don't worry, you share 80% of your brain,
Out I came with a cry,
But I saw you with an open eye,
You are a mother,
Like no other,
While staying with you, I happily grew;
All I want to say is, I love you!

Sarah Muraj (13)
Bentley Wood High School, Stanmore

If Kids Ruled The World...

If kids ruled the world adults would go to school,
Kids would be the teachers and rule.
Every month there would be a holiday,
Perfect time to get away.

If kids ruled the world they would be wealthy,
Adults would have no choice but to be healthy.
For breakfast adults would have gruel,
That makes kids very cruel.

If kids ruled the world it would be full of candy,
Whereas adults would go to school with a bottle of brandy.
Gadgets would be very good,
Everyone would live in a great neighbourhood.

Aneya Shah (11)
Bentley Wood High School, Stanmore

Earth

The Earth needs you to change your way,
Month by month and day by day.
Single-use plastic lasts almost forever;
It might be cheap but not very clever.

When you see litter on the streets,
And the air smells of pollution,
When you feel like it's piling up,
Remember there is a solution.

The changes are easy, just look and you'll see
The difference that can be made is by you and me.
It can end up in oceans, rivers and seas;
The wind sometimes carries it and it gets tangled in the trees.

Iklas Haashi (11)
Bentley Wood High School, Stanmore

Water Falling

W ater falling from the trees
A nd lakes drifting through the breeze
T ogether the waves sail the seas
E arth turns to mud
R epitles hide beneath the water.

F rogs hopping on lily pads
A nd water falls like tears from the sky
L eaves collapse from the trees
L aying under the dead branches
I magine if you were a mermaid
N o one disturbs you as you lay peacefully
G rey sky above you.

Jaimisha Patel (12)
Bentley Wood High School, Stanmore

The Dream

Waking up in my crisp clean sheets one morning,
Something strange was about to happen, giving me no warning.

I quickly got dressed in the cold, silent darkness,
My eyes not adjusting, just waiting for the sharpness.

Once I could see straight I opened the door,
Wondering what confusion I was about to explore.

I ate my breakfast one piece at a time with nobody around,
Then I set off to school dragging my feet on the ground.

First it was a posh and nicely dressed lady that I saw,
She looked at me for a second and said, "Bonjour."

Wait... that sounded crazy. Are my ears failing me?
No, it must have been the blowing wind past the tree.

Shaking my head I looked up and saw my cousin,
In a crowded gang there was probably a dozen.

I waved at them and started walking closer to the flock,
Then heard something weird from around the block.

It was Mr Wilkes my favourite teacher,
But wait, why can't I understand the words from this creature?

Am I dreaming or on another planet? This doesn't feel cool.
Then I saw Paris written in big letters at the top of the school.

Not being able to understand anybody that day,
Was the scariest time that I didn't want to replay.

I then found myself mysterious being woken up by my mum...
Had this really been a dream? I felt really dumb!

Ava Mae Holland (11)
Cansfield High School, Ashton-in-Makerfield

Imagine The Future

I magine being able to see people's future and on January 1st 2020 seeing nothing for anybody.

M aybe something was wrong. Thinking that it was because you're a little tired you get an early night.

A fter waking up feeling refreshed, nothing has changed. Everybody still has no future, you start to panic but who can you tell? Nobody knows about your ability...

G oing on each month faster and faster of quarantine, the virus begins to spread even more affecting more countries daily. You start to worry that you will never see family or friends again. You wonder if anybody will have a future...

I t began to get worse. The virus was in every country and it was killing people who caught it. It terrified everyone that the deaths wouldn't stop.

N ext, began to the protest of Black Lives Matter after George Floyd was killed on the streets.

E verything and everybody was falling apart. People were losing hope of ever being able to go outside and have fun. Stuck in their houses like a prisoner in a cell.

Megan Pearce (11)
Cansfield High School, Ashton-in-Makerfield

What Would It Be Like To Live In A Movie?

What would it be like to live in a movie?
Maybe it would be really groovy.
Maybe I would be a star
Or I wouldn't go very far.
Would the characters be really nice
Or would they have a heart as cold as ice?
Maybe the movie would be really fun
Or the complicated problems are never done.
Would I stand in the centre of a scene to be listened to and seen?
Will it be comedy, horror, adventure or action?
Will it be full of satisfaction?
Will I be good or bad?
Will I be happy or sad?
Will there be truth?
Will there be lies?
Will there be lots of people left to die?
Will I be on a loyal friendly team
Or will there be lots of shouts and screams?
Will the world be dirt and grease
Or will it be full of peace?
I wonder... Wait! Can you actually be in a movie?
Is it true?
If it is, what will I do?

Katie Naylor (11)
Cansfield High School, Ashton-in-Makerfield

The Life Of An Angel

Imagine an angel falls from the sky,
You don't think much of it,
You see shooting stars almost every other night.
But something draws you away, from your homework,
Even though it's due in the next day.
There is a bright light in the distance,
It makes you ponder your own existence.
Is life really worth living
Or is it just endlessly unforgiving?
As you reach the crater you look inside,
There is something greater.
"An angel!" you cry, you observe its torn off wings
And it can no longer fly.
It's a spirit from beyond, you try talking to it,
But it won't respond.
There it is, that light again,
But where was it that you saw it then?
It's coming for you and you realise your death is due.
You regret not doing more, with the angel you will join,
Lying dead on the floor.

Ben Sudworth (12)
Cansfield High School, Ashton-in-Makerfield

Imagine If...

I magine if I was a big fluffy dog,
F rolicking through the long green, sharp grass.

I would curl into a ball and rest my head in front of the hot, burning fireplace.

W et, soggy smudges made by my big black nose.
A lways on the hunt for some delicious food to munch.
S oft and smooth paws gently rest on my owner's hand.

A s my piercing blue eyes gaze out of the window fiercely, the world passes by.

P layfully biting my owner as we fight.
O verly giddy, I could accidentally hurt the ones I love.
M anoeuvring my body like a lion hunting for its prey.
S niffing the fresh air with my twitching nose.
K issing and licking, morning till night.
Y awning and sleeping the day away.

Max Woosey (11)
Cansfield High School, Ashton-in-Makerfield

Imagine If The World Was A Game Of Monopoly

Imagine if the world was just a massive game of Monopoly...

You would have bank errors in your favour
When usually it would be the other way round.
You would have mass serial killers,
Who could get out of jail for free with just a simple card.
You would never know if you're going to college or university,
You can't do anything about it as it is predicted by the roll of the dice...

Serial killers and evil people would be able to keep committing crimes and getting out of jail too.
Money would be at a higher income.

If the world a game of Monopoly,
Most likely no one would have gone through wars and viruses.
No world hunger and most people would have a home.
Would the world be better as Monopoly or not?

Jake Pimblett (12)
Cansfield High School, Ashton-in-Makerfield

If I Was My Favourite

If she was her favourite, she would be a flower,
If he was his favourite, he would be a tower.
That one over there, they'd become a light,
My friend across the street, he'd definitely be a paper that's white.

Me, on the other hand, now it's something interesting,
You would judge me if I said it, as fast as lightning.
Now hold on to your statement, don't raise a hand,
To me, my favourite isn't as big as all this land.

If I were my favourite, it would be a cold-breathing maniac,
Two eyes full of madness and a bit of a brainiac.
Dust stitched all over his clothes and a grin so slim,
I'd tell you my favourite, but it's too ridiculous for you.

Wojciech Pozniak (12)
Cansfield High School, Ashton-in-Makerfield

Imagine If We Could Design Who We Are

D esign. Everyone can create who they are and how they want to be.

E bullient. People will finally start liking themselves because they are beautiful.

S elf-love. People will finally start liking themselves instead of hating themselves.

I dol. People will stop looking up to their idols because their idols are prettier than them.

G aiety. People will start showing more gaiety as they will be their own type of perfect.

N onchalant. People will be nonchalant because they will not have to worry about being perfect.

S pread this message because you are

A mazing just the way you are.

Y ou are your own type of perfect and always just be you.

Grace Cannon (12)
Cansfield High School, Ashton-in-Makerfield

Imagine It

Imagine if you were put in some crazy situation
And had to pick between two different choices.
But when you imagine it more
Would you start to change your mind?
Imagine if you could have any superpower you wanted,
Would you like to know what people think about you?
Which superpower would you have?
Imagine if kids also ruled the world.
I wonder what it would be like,
Some people think it is going to happen.
Anyone can imagine anything they want to,
Just keep believing and imagine all that you can.
Imagine if something crazy happened,
How would it make you feel or even how others feel?
When you find out,
Start to imagine anything you can.

Lottie Walsh (12)
Cansfield High School, Ashton-in-Makerfield

Imagine If You Could...

Imagine if you could stop racism,
People would not be scared to come out of their house,
People would not be treated differently,
People would not be killed or hurt because of their colour.

Imagine if you could stop pollution,
The Earth would be a much better place,
Animals would be much better and stop dying,
The ozone layer would mend itself.

Imagine if you could stop war,
People could live in peace,
People would not be scared,
People would feel happy and safe.

Imagine if you could stop world hunger,
People would not starve,
People would not be hungry,
People would be much happier.

Faye Lawson (11)
Cansfield High School, Ashton-in-Makerfield

Inside A Computer Game

C omputer games, they're such a trick
O ne cool thing is they're gone with a click
M y thoughts swirl around my head
P lus I wonder if my friends are dead
U nlike me they're not trapped in a game
T hat is because they thought they were lame
E nded up being good for them
R eally I'm trapped in a game called Gurklegem

G o find the fiery sword inside the maze
A nd set the dragon into a heating blaze
M y family will be waiting for me to come back to Rome
E ventually I will escape and get back home.

Harry Paterson (12)
Cansfield High School, Ashton-in-Makerfield

Imagine If You Could Fly

Imagine if you could fly,
You could fly as high as planes,
Imagine how many places you could go to or see,
Or you could even meet people you would never have thought you would meet before,
Swooping in and out of buildings and people,
You would never have to pay for a plane ticket again or taxi,
How cool would it be to fly your girlfriend to the top of the Empire State Building at Christmas?
You could even fly all around the world,
Visiting all the famous landmarks,
Just imagine how nice it would be soaring through the air,
Swerving in and out of buildings,
Imagine if you could fly...

Theo Leyland (12)
Cansfield High School, Ashton-in-Makerfield

My Imagination Poem

Imagine if you were in a rocket about to ascend into space.
Imagine if the rocket broke down in space.
Imagine floating to a different solar system.
Imagine seeing all of the new planets that have never been seen.
Imagine being the only person ever to go to a different solar system.
Now imagine floating back to our solar system and seeing our planets.
Imagine seeing hundreds and thousands of stars.
Now imagine being crowded by everyone shouting, "She's back, she's back."
Now imagine if that was all just a dream.

Katie Jones (12)
Cansfield High School, Ashton-in-Makerfield

Imagine, Imagine

Imagine, imagine,
If all of the games you played came true,
If you were a part of it,
Maybe in a battlefield fighting a war,
Or in an F1 car racing to get 1st place.
Imagine, imagine,
If the game was playing you,
If you were the players not them,
Making you do all of these things.
Imagine, imagine,
If the Monopoly character you lost was you,
In the dark abyss of loneliness.
Imagine, imagine,
That game you never play
Compared to the game you don't play.
Imagine, imagine.

Jack Mannion (11)
Cansfield High School, Ashton-in-Makerfield

What Is It Like To Control Someone?

What is it like to control someone?
Is it funny and weird
Or is it very entertaining?
Oh how I wonder what it's like.
Would I ruin someone's life
Or would I make it better?
Only if I knew.
Would I make them fly to space
Or would I make them travel the world?
Would they ever meet me?
Would we even become friends
Or would we be enemies?
Oh how I wonder.
Would they thank me?
Would they hate me
Or would they love me.
Oh how I wonder what it would be like...

Lilly-Mae Robson (12)
Cansfield High School, Ashton-in-Makerfield

Lies

Imagine if you couldn't lie,
Some of you would love it,
But others would rather die,
Imagine if you couldn't lie.

There would be no need for politicians you see,
Harder to commit crimes,
How much better the world would be,
Imagine if you couldn't lie.

There may be a bad side about never lying,
You might upset your friends and they might upset you
And they may not forgive you no matter how hard you try,
Imagine if you couldn't lie.

Mia Blackwood (11)
Cansfield High School, Ashton-in-Makerfield

The Titans Are Here

The Titans are here,
How can we be safe?
Our homes will be destroyed,
Can we be saved?

These bloodthirsty monsters
They have to be gone.
But how can we stop them?
We have to be strong.

A few years later huge walls have been built,
Built to protect us.
Yes, they do help a lot,
But when they are breached the scouts are sent off.

The scouts have to have courage,
They give up their own lives
So all else can survive.

Poppy Goulding (11)
Cansfield High School, Ashton-in-Makerfield

Eat, Sleep, Repeat

The alarm goes off,
You open your eyes.
The weather so bright,
What a surprise.

You have a strange feeling as you step out your bedroom door,
It feels very familiar,
Like you have done this before.

As you look outside the landing window,
The light is so very bright.
The sun is reflecting strongly.
The ground is covered in white.

This feels like a memory you already had,
Like you did this yesterday,
Are you going mad?

Emma Pimblett (11)
Cansfield High School, Ashton-in-Makerfield

What If...

The world could be a better place
If people put a smile on their face.
Imagine if kids ruled the world,
How would that feel in the morning as they uncurl?
Imagine if they could see the real you
Watching slowly as you grow.
Imagine if you could change history,
It would all go to the big mystery
Or would you erase the bad?
However that could make some mad.
So spread a bit of kindness everywhere you go,
Even if it's just a polite hello.

Abbie Jones (12)
Cansfield High School, Ashton-in-Makerfield

Imagine Being Immortal

I magine being immortal, careful you must be with your choice.
M any people I have seen come and go.
M emories, too many I have gained.
O ne day, the dark will come, afraid I am not.
R oaming the streets which were once full.
T ales of more than a thousand years and still plenty more to come.
A t last the time is near.
L onely and drifting in space with only stars and planets around to watch.

Daylan Sleigh-Geary (12)
Cansfield High School, Ashton-in-Makerfield

Imagine What Christmas Is Like

December is here,
Christmas is near.
Snow is falling
As the fire is roaring.
Lights are twinkling
As the tinsel is glistening.
People are shopping
And the crackers are popping.
The choir is singing
As the stockings are hanging.
Santa's food is laying
While the reindeer are sleighing.
The presents are playful
And the family is joyful.
Merry Christmas everyone.

Emily Pollitt (11)
Cansfield High School, Ashton-in-Makerfield

Tropical Paradise

Everyone gets along well,
People look at the shells,
People spend the day on a tropical beach,
The palm trees are singing,
The people are dancing,
No problems for this tropical paradise.
Don't need police,
Don't need hospitality,
What a tropical life,
You're living the dream
Out on this tropical beach.
One small bit of land,
All your wishes have come true.

Oliver Hodge (11)
Cansfield High School, Ashton-in-Makerfield

Alone

Everyone is gone.
Our town is completely vacant.
What happened?
As you think that you're alone,
You are wrong.

You think to yourself,
Am I dreaming?
It isn't a dream, it's reality.
People are searching the discarded homes of the town.
Although they aren't humans,
They're bloodthirsty demons.

Alesha Parr (11)
Cansfield High School, Ashton-in-Makerfield

Horrible History

H orrible things that happened in the past
I magine if you could change that
S o many sad things but sometimes good
T error fell all over
O h how sad to see such sorrow
R emember the people who risked their lives
Y oung and old people who have died.

Esmé Skinner (12)
Cansfield High School, Ashton-in-Makerfield

Imagine If Dreams Were Real

Imagine if dreams were real,
Imagine if dreams came true.
Even though some dreams do,
Imagine if dreams were real.
Imagine sleeping,
You suddenly start weeping.
You had a bad dream
That made you scream.
It's not a big deal,
Because dreams aren't real.

Summer Bell (11)
Cansfield High School, Ashton-in-Makerfield

I Wish I Could Fly

I wish I could fly in the night sky,
Soaring with the birds,
I hope I don't die.
Over the seas, mountains as well,
I hope I don't bump into a seagull again.
I wish I could fly up to a star,
And make a wish upon a star.
I wish I could fly.

Isabelle Nisbet (11)
Cansfield High School, Ashton-in-Makerfield

Imagine If...

Imagine if humans disappeared.
Imagine if all oceans were cleared.
Imagine if the animals were extinct.
Imagine if all the plants got a disease.
Imagine if robots ruled.
Imagine if the world was destroyed.

Leo Pimblett (11)
Cansfield High School, Ashton-in-Makerfield

Colossal Carnage

I was woken by a flash,
Everywhere was bright,
I got up in a dash,
The horizon was white.

An asteroid hit Earth,
The ground shuddered violently,
The explosion had loud girth,
Boulders flew all around me.

I stepped outside,
Into the powerful wind,
People were swiftly dying,
Rubble blew over the Mynd.

A gale made me fly backwards,
My body hit a tree,
This caused me to get plastered,
With bark from head to knee.

As I finally stood up straight,
Sand blew into my eyes,
I felt like I would faint,
I didn't want to die!

At the last moment,
I took cover behind a car,

I was far from enjoyment,
On my face I'd got a scar.

I'd had enough,
This had to stop.
I really wasn't that tough,
This wind needed to drop.

In my last breaths,
I struggled to survive.
This was my inevitable death,
Now came my short demise.

Camren Farrington-Hyrons (11)
Oldbury Wells School, Bridgnorth

If Children Rule The World

Imagine if we could rule the world,
There would never be a telling word.

Parents would go and do as they please,
While we sit indoors and munch on cheese.

No more Michael Gove,
Homework would have to go.

Pens and paper would not exist,
Computer games would be top of the list.

Household chores will never be seen,
I could do as I please and just be me.

Let's face it, it will never work, this idea is too bold,
Let's wait and see what the future holds!

Dylan Hill (12)
Oldbury Wells School, Bridgnorth

Big Cats Of The Savannah

I watch the cubs playfight,
Beside the camouflaging bushes,
Before them the savannah's light,
Seated on their tushes,
The lionesses look on,
Towards a job well done,
Into the distance upon,
The males swiftly kill one.

The cheetahs run in a race,
To catch appetising antelope,
An attempt without a trace,
They abandon all its hope,
With the kill underlooked,
They guard their meal,
Walking home as thunder shakes,
With food of a great deal.

Benjamin Jordan (12)
Oldbury Wells School, Bridgnorth

Nightmare?

Knocking on the window,
In the dead of night,
Howling winds circled,
They whispered, "Don't let the bed bugs bite!"

Big brown eyes,
Swaying side to side,
"Open your eyes!" they chanted
As I attempted to hide.

Small white figures,
Shone before my eyes,
Bony fingers
Waved their goodbyes.

As two white fingers,
Blood dripping from their bones,
Shone before me,
My skin as cold as stone.

Anna Cole (13)
Oldbury Wells School, Bridgnorth

Animation

My animations bring me joy,
They make me calm and content,
It's like the pen moves by itself,
The ink stains my fingers,
The workplace is so lively, erupting with ideas,
And though I do so like the help, I need a little quiet,
As the end of the day comes near,
There comes a beautiful moment,
I see my drawings come to life,
Upon the shining screen,
And then they dance and sing so merrily,
As I smile so wearily.

Kimberley Kendall (12)
Oldbury Wells School, Bridgnorth

If Pets Could Talk!

If pets could talk, what would they say?
They would be able to tell us if they wanted to play
And say, "Let me off my lead, I promise I won't run away!"
They'd be able to tell us if they'd had a good day
Tell us what they wanted for tea
And what they really think of me!
If pets could talk my life would be great
And then my dog would really be my best mate!

Nyima Winters (12)
Oldbury Wells School, Bridgnorth

Land Is Vast

The grass is long
The poppies grow
In Flanders Field the memories flow

The muddy water
The low stock of food
Someone dies in front of your eyes

No Man's Land is silent at last
No one here and the land is vast

The birds chirp and the war is over,
Until we meet again I will remember you always.

Lydia Walker (12)
Oldbury Wells School, Bridgnorth

Imagine If Kids Ruled The World

I f kids ruled the world it would be a disaster
M ums would have to cook and clean all day
A nd we would play all day
G randmas would get fed up
I would be lying in bed with my hurting head
N o one would have to go to work
E veryone would lurk

I f kids ruled the world it would be a disaster
F our to five-year-old kids will scream and shout

K ids would make their mum pout
I will be eating all day
D ads would have to work all day
S ausages will be a feast, we will gorge and guzzle like a beast

R ock stars normally sing, but now they will ring
U mbrellas would not be for rain, but to hit your vein
L ED lights will now be whips, not to worry waiters will tip
E verything is ending
D on't be scared.

Haajarah Tahir (12)
Ormiston Horizon Academy, Tunstall

Imagine - Without Imagining

They say eyes are the window to the soul,
But mine rather work like a bowl.
Collects all the grey,
Never expelling anything out.
But what 'thing' would I be, if my soul had a drought?

Just imagine quite closely
Eye-to-eye, ear-to-ear.
Imagine never having feelings - imagine controlling all the fear.
Imagine a canvas - dripping with paint,
Covered in a chromatic symphony of rose gold, yellow, purple, pink.
Such an aesthetic wonderland that just makes you think.

The world bending around you, shape-shifting at your command.
Everyone kneeling before you, life's greatest at your hand.
My eyes have no window - I bolted it shut,
No pity, no sympathy and I can't even feel a cut.
My soul is no longer crispy or cool or calm.
Every scar I once adorned now simply locates in my palm.

Gracie Harris (13)
Ormiston Horizon Academy, Tunstall

Lost Forever

It's a regular day,
Just me alone,
My friends and family non-existent,
I sit in my scrap shed in the supermarket,
It's a good source of food, but it is quite mouldy,
You're wondering why, I'll tell you.
The world's barren and humans were abducted,
But not me, I survived,
I do my daily routine and forage for scraps.
Today was good, I made a friend, it's a mouse,
Unfortunately it eats me out of home
So I kicked the little rascal out.
I doze off in my bug-ridden mattress,
Half asleep I see a star-shaped UFO
Zoom above my head, so I rush up and run,
Sprinting like my life depends on it and I realise it's a star.
I remember I'm alone and need to accept it.
I go back to my hut, only to notice
The little mouse devouring my cheese.

Finley Sawyer (12)
Ormiston Horizon Academy, Tunstall

Imagine If Your Friend Was A Vampire

Imagine if your friend was a vampire,
She would suck your blood.
It would leave a really big mark,
Well it could.
Imagine if your friend was a vampire.

Imagine if your friend was a vampire,
She would turn into a bat, to get to school.
Imagine if your friend was a vampire.

Imagine if your friend was a vampire,
She would never be seen in a picture,
Or in a mirror, imagine being a killer.
Imagine if your friend was a vampire.

Imagine if your friend was a vampire,
She would have pale skin
And blend in a white wall.
Imagine if your friend was a vampire.

Imagine if your friend was a vampire,
She could fly away into the dark sky,
Imagine if your friend was a vampire.

Charlotte Plant (11)
Ormiston Horizon Academy, Tunstall

Afterlife

Afterlife is mysterious in all different ways,
Heaven, hell, limbo is what others say.
People have different beliefs and that's okay,
Maybe the Devil will say hey.
Pagan, Satanic, Christian, who cares? They chatter
But as long as they are happy it doesn't matter.
Even if your beliefs are beyond, afar,
You are who you are.
We have the right to believe and imagine what we want.
Just don't go and taunt.
Seeing people doing what their God asks,
They imagine this will get them into Heaven, even if it means wearing a mask.
People doing what they should,
This shows they can get anywhere, they imagine they really could.
The point is it shouldn't matter what you imagine,
Even if it is Latin.

Lexi Ashmall (13)
Ormiston Horizon Academy, Tunstall

Imagine

What a night for me, scoring goals and goals,
But wait, something has followed me, the door is open.
"Mum," I say... No response.
As I get scared I run down to the basement
And... "Argh!" I scream.
My mum is kidnapped in the basement.
Stomp, stomp, stomp,
OMG, it's a monster.
I run as fast as I can outside the door...
"Oh no, I haven't got my phone," I whimper.
I turn my body as it is standing there staring,
It chases me as I go to the police station,
But no one's there,
I run into a jail cell and hide,
The monster doesn't have a face,
The face opens at my cell and then...
"Wake up Pete," says my mum.

Jack Vickers (11)
Ormiston Horizon Academy, Tunstall

I Will Never Forget

I will never forget when I scored the

W inning goal,
I n front of 1,600 people. It was the most amazing day of my
L ife, I was so happy about it. I
L oved it, could take that away from me,

N o one,
E ven if they tried, my team was screaming
V ery loud, it felt like I
E ntered New York, it was that loud
R eality got the best of me though,

F or I didn't believe it was reality but I wasn't sure,
O r if it was fake,
R eally fake, I
G ot suspicious that it was a dream,
E ventually I woke up but I will never forget
T he glory.

Henry Hughes (11)
Ormiston Horizon Academy, Tunstall

Imagine

I opened my eyes to see dinosaurs going to fly,
Oh and a T-rex passing by.
Petting little dinosaurs which were as friendly as can be,
One's climbing high and dropping branches from a tree.
I saw ones fighting together in water
And little lambs going to be slaughtered.
A dino called me to take me up in the sky,
I felt so free and I touched the clouds which were so dry.
I was placed back down onto the ground,
I ran straight until I saw a cave that's never been found.
I looked in the cave to see many bats,
I screamed without sound as I saw the rats.
Running out with all my fear,
I stopped dead to see I was greeted by a bear.

Ava Harvey-Gibson (12)
Ormiston Horizon Academy, Tunstall

World Cup Final

Scoring in the World Cup final is a dream.
I want to play for the England first team.
Even playing in the World Cup for England is a dream.
In the changing rooms we can have a laugh and a scream.
I've always wanted to go professional
And I also want to meet Wayne Rooney.
But I will have to work hard and stick to football.
I don't want to be a goalkeeper like Nick Pope
Or a defender like Virgil van Dijk,
I want to be a forward like Marcus Rashford.
I can imagine the feeling of scoring the winner in the World Cup final.
It must be amazing, the crowd will go wild
And I will be all over social media.

Josh Duncan (12)
Ormiston Horizon Academy, Tunstall

If Aliens Exist...

I know it's weird but what if aliens attacked,
F rantically running about like they own the place?

A t last we saw them.
L azily we did nothing to stop them!
I would hide,
E ven if they could find me, what would they look like?
N evertheless I wouldn't be worried,
S urprisingly I thought that they would be nice.

E ven though it's not real, what if they had...
X -ray vision!
I t's impossible but... it's cool!
S uddenly I wake up and think,
T ime is running out - what is this is real?

Delilah May Brough (12)
Ormiston Horizon Academy, Tunstall

The Perks Of Life

Imagine if you were immortal
You could live forever on
Doing as you wish
But having to watch your loved ones move on.

Imagine if you were immortal
You could seek so much revenge
For those who turned against you
Will never see the end.

Imagine if you were immortal
You wouldn't understand
The amazing parts of life
For the perks go hand-in-hand.

Thank goodness for the existence of life
Now I know it is important
That sometimes it's good to die
I've never thought about this before
But now life and death is what we should cherish a little more.

Aimeé-Grace Shaw (13)
Ormiston Horizon Academy, Tunstall

Just A Nightmare

J ust a nightmare, that's all it is
U nimaginable things coming to life
S omething tickling my feet
T hen hiding right back under my bed

A nightmare, that's all it is

N othing to worry about
I magine unicorns and fairies and all those magical things
G ood thoughts
H appy thoughts
T ime is ticking
M inutes then it will all be over
A couple of minutes, that's all, that's it
R eally close, you'll wake up soon
E verything will be over, a nightmare that's all it is.

Esme West (11)
Ormiston Horizon Academy, Tunstall

What Is Normal Anyway?

Imagine if I could live my life
Like any other child,
I'm 'normal' on the inside,
What is normal anyway?

"You're not like us," they chant,
But I only want to play,
"It doesn't matter, you're not normal."
What is normal anyway?

"Look at my new toy," I said.
"Eww, that's gross," exclaimed they.
I only wanted this toy because it's normal,
What is normal anyway?

What is normal can I ask?
Imagine if I was normal,
I could play with all the children,
Again I ask, what is normal anyway?

Millie Rafferty (12)
Ormiston Horizon Academy, Tunstall

Imagine...

Imagine being bullied.
Bullying, don't do it.
They laugh, they giggle,
They keep on doing it until tears run down your face.
Made fun of if I cry.
Been spoken about too many times.
I'd had enough and I would cry.
I didn't know what to do or say.
I was too scared to trust anyone.
Cyberbullied, face-to-face bullied,
Fighting to hold back tears.
I finally found my confidence but then lost it again.
Wondering why I'm not enough,
Anxiety, depression, insecurity, heartbroken,
They got the better of me but then
I made friends with them but they did it again...

Ruby-Mai Mountford (12)
Ormiston Horizon Academy, Tunstall

The Girl Behind The Mask (Imagine If No One Knew It Was You)

A shy, quiet, sensible child,
The type to be anything but wild,
But when her foot hits that stage
And the spotlight shines on her face,
Her personality breaks free of the cage
And the quiet girl has gone without a trace.

Her arms and legs moving together,
If only she could do this forever.
"Who is the girl behind the mask?"
She hears the thousands of people ask.
The last move in the dance and the audience roars,
Congratulating her with rounds of applause,
They long to know, they long to ask,
But for now, she will be 'the girl in the mask'.

Millie Elson (13)
Ormiston Horizon Academy, Tunstall

Wishes

I   f I had three wishes
F inally I could have what I want

I would be happy

H ave you ever imagined it?
A ll would be good
D ying, I couldn't die

T he animals could talk
H appy life
R ampaging animals
E verything would be fun
E very animal would be free

W hat should I wish for?
I should wish for no war
S hould I wish for something else?
H elp me decide
E ven I can't hide
S hould I wish for everything?

Brian Boulton (12)
Ormiston Horizon Academy, Tunstall

Imagine

S coring that goal
E cstasy bubbling out of you
C limbing to your feet
"U p, we are going up,"
R oared the Ultras
I n the Boothen End
N ever stopping
G ame, set and match Stoke City.

P itch invasions followed
R aucous noise filling the city
O nly this club
M akes me this happy
O nly this club!
T om Smith with the goal
I nfuriated away fans disappeared
O utstanding performance from the boys
N ever stop believing.

Tom Smith (13)
Ormiston Horizon Academy, Tunstall

Imagine If...

Imagine if people knew the real you.
Scary, isn't it?

Imagine all the stares you'd get.
Imagine what people would think of you.

Imagine them knowing you put on a mask.
Imagine them knowing that you were under attack
From the thoughts that kept you awake at night,
From the thoughts that you knew would bite.

Imagine them knowing the real you.
The fighter you are
And the things you can do.

Imagine them knowing the person you are,
The people you'll go on to help
And the world you'll change as you are.

Elise Robinson (13)
Ormiston Horizon Academy, Tunstall

Imagine If You Could See...

T he future whatever it beholds we could never predict, but what if you could?
H ow would you use this power? What would you see?
E very possible outcome to something you could see.

F eeling, having the feeling and power to basically know anything that's going to happen next.
U nbelievable. Would any new animals appear?
T errifying. What would happen to the world?
U nimaginable. could there be flying cars?
R egretting our decisions, animals and rainforests are gone.
E verything is destroyed and empty.

Vanessa Popko (11)
Ormiston Horizon Academy, Tunstall

Imagine

Imagine if everyone was equal,
In films, most wouldn't have a prequel.
Imagine if they knew the real you,
Who else would know, would you know too?
Imagine if you could see the future -
Then I'd write it up on a computer.
Imagine if dreams were real.
All the things I could go touch and feel.
Imagine if the world was about to end -
Then there would be nothing to defend.
Imagine if you had one wish -
To have the most expensive meal or dish.
Imagine if we were in a computer game -
Then we would have to use a gun and aim.

Evan Kinsey (12)
Ormiston Horizon Academy, Tunstall

Imagine If...

Imagine if I were famous.
Imagine if I was a gymnast.
Imagine if I were a model.
Imagine if I was magic.
Imagine if I was a fish.
Imagine if I was small.
Imagine if I were a TV presenter.
Imagine if I was rich.
Imagine if I was a teacher.
Imagine if I was the Queen.
Imagine if I was an author.
Imagine if I was an actress.
Imagine if I was a murderer.
Imagine if I weren't here.
Imagine if I was immortal.
Imagine if I were supernatural.
Imagine if I was a police person.
Imagine if I weren't me.

Megan Nixon (14)
Ormiston Horizon Academy, Tunstall

Game Over

Imagine if we were avatars in a computer game.
Imagine if nothing mattered because you could change time,
Let other people take the blame
For your wrongdoings and crimes.
This life is pure carnage,
Every unneeded save slot goes to the garbage.

But the game is slowly fading away now,
What is the point of 'living'?
Time for the pixels last bow,
For this life is surely not giving,
I feel like giving up
Like the last drop of an emptying cup.

For the game is over now,
It is time to say goodnight.

Grace Leigh (12)
Ormiston Horizon Academy, Tunstall

If Aliens Exist

I may be seeing an alien
F or the first time in history

A fter all this time there couldn't be one alive
L ife couldn't be possible beyond Earth, could it?
I magine seeing an alien
E xisting on Planet Earth
N ot only seeing humans
S eeing their new inventions

E ating new types of food
X -ray vision can finally be invented
I magine seeing an alien
S o where is he from?
T o the moons and stars where they are from.

Ryan Colclough (13)
Ormiston Horizon Academy, Tunstall

If Aliens Exist

I f aliens flew down to Earth
F iring their weapons

A rocket was flying, people were
L ying on the floor, because they were sadly hit by a door
I ntimidating aliens landing on the floor, with a door gun
E lon Musk our saviour
N eutralised the aliens with a Tesla
S ent them back to their pathetic planet, I was just

E ating a sandwich
X avia was scared
I n her house, a door
S ent her flying
T he aliens are gone forever.

Patrick Chapinski (13)
Ormiston Horizon Academy, Tunstall

If Aliens Exist

I f I saw an alien
F lying through the sky

A live they might be
L ike a horror movie, that is what it appeared to me
I was taken by surprise
E xtra fear came to me when I saw their leader
N ot what you'd expect
S uppose they are dangerous

E xtraordinary weaponry, never seen before
X -ray vision they have
I think they might be nice
S ince they have not killed me yet but
T he rest is yet to happen.

Jensen Grocott (13)
Ormiston Horizon Academy, Tunstall

Imagine

Imagine if we lived forever...
Imagine if we could fly...
Imagine if dragons were real...
Imagine if we could teleport...
Imagine if kids ran the world...
Imagine if unicorns were real...
Imagine if dreams came true...
Imagine if you had infinite wishes...
Imagine if pets could live forever...
Imagine if science could cure anything...
Imagine if we could time travel...
Imagine if you were a millionaire...
Imagine if nightmares were real...
Imagine if everything you want came to life.

Ellie-Mae Condliffe (12)
Ormiston Horizon Academy, Tunstall

What's In The Future?

S ad and happy times to see.
E normous changes past belief.
E xtinction of humans or what to expect.

T he terrifying future, what's coming next?
H ard times, a lot like a knock on the head.
E xpressive emotions from the dead.

F rom the sky we may live.
U nstable beasts in the mist.
T ransport from no other thing,
U sing boats with moving wings.
R emedies that can cure us now,
E xcept how?

Lillie Jones (12)
Ormiston Horizon Academy, Tunstall

You're The Only Person Left

Imagine if you're the only person left,
As if everyone just poofed out of your head.
I'd roam the streets, scared and alone,
Retrieving the past and humans.

a vermillion soul appeared before my eyes,
Its eyes were fair; as if they never told lies.
It held out a hand,
No sign of fear.

I grabbed it and disappeared
With the figure.

So imagine if you were in such a world…
Would you grab the spirit's hand
Or shape the past by yourself?

Aleksandra Grosiak (12)
Ormiston Horizon Academy, Tunstall

Imagine

Imagine a world where all can be one.
Imagine a world where no one needs a gun.
Imagine a world where no one needs drugs.
Just a world where you need a hug.

A world where anything can happen,
All you have to do is imagine.
Imagine if these dreams were actually real,
All I have to do is lay on my pillow,
Just imagine how amazing that would feel.

To know that you will be safe,
Tucked up in bed
With not a worry,
Just imagine a world where all can be one.

Amber Louise Pateman (13)
Ormiston Horizon Academy, Tunstall

If Aliens Exist

I   magine seeing an alien
F   amilies and families

A   round their planet.
L   aughing and playing
I   n each other's houses
E   ating all their favourite foods in the
N   ever-ending space.
S   ome are happy and some are sad

E   ven some are bad.
X   -ray vision seeing through planets, even Earth
I   ncluding watching birth.
S   taring at spaceships flying by
T   o and from Earth in the sky.

Evan Jones (12)
Ormiston Horizon Academy, Tunstall

This Is America

Black lives matter
Protests on every corner
Discrimination everywhere
This is America.
Get paid your job to give for your health
It's just living, why is it anything else?
This is America.
Dress codes and bullies
School shootings everywhere
This is America.
All we do is swear
Body shaming
Transphobia, homophobia
Colour discrimination
It's okay
This is America.
The worst country of the year
Do you still want to come here?

Emily Jane Harris (13)
Ormiston Horizon Academy, Tunstall

Imagine If Dreams Were Real...

I like sleeping
In my bed
With dreams and thoughts wandering through my head.

Imagine if these dreams were real
As I lay on my pillow
How amazing would that feel?

The warmth and comfort these dreams bring to me,
What if that could be our new reality?
That is how I want life to be.

I could finally remember every dream,
Each one a brand-new memory,
How simple does this seem?

With dreams and thoughts wandering through my head.

Emma Davis (13)
Ormiston Horizon Academy, Tunstall

Imagine If You Were Immortal

I'm 12 years old,
I'm going to see everything
And I'm going to live forever.

I'm 20 years old,
I've stopped ageing,
It's nice living forever.

I'm 50 years old,
My mum has died,
I'm living forever.

I'm 120 years old,
They're all almost gone,
I'm not sure if I want to live forever.

I'm 230 years old,
I'm all alone
And I don't want to live forever.

Lexie Jones (12)
Ormiston Horizon Academy, Tunstall

Imagine If...

Imagine if we used to live on Mars,
We would have lived among the greatest stars,
But we killed it due to pollution
And there was only one solution.

Send two people to another planet,
In an escape pod,
Imagine it.

Imagine if they landed on Earth.
A completely new turf,
But the impact was so large,
It killed all of the dinosaurs.

These two people were Adam and Eve,
Sent by God to restore humanity,
Imagine it.

Brendan Dawson (13)
Ormiston Horizon Academy, Tunstall

My Amazing Alien

I had encountered an alien
F or fun we played

A mong us the new
L IT game everyone's talking about
I really want to be the imposter.
E lon Musk rang me up, so did
N ASA, they really wanted to
S ee my amazing discovery.

E ven my mum rang,
X ylophone screams
I n their planet,
S aturn has gone far,
T ill I see you again, bye-bye alien.

Jack Hardy (13)
Ormiston Horizon Academy, Tunstall

Imagine If You Could Make A Change

What if everything just froze.
What if you could make a change.
Completely demolish a pigeon shooting range.

Clear the plastic from the ocean
Without causing an utter commotion.
What if you could stop a burning
Building, the flames paused in their churning.
What if you saved a turtle
And for some reason called it Myrtle.

What if you stopped global warming
Just after all these warnings.
What if you could make a change.

Lucy Batho (13)
Ormiston Horizon Academy, Tunstall

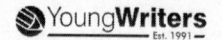

What Are Aliens Like?

Out in space
There could be a whole new race
Maybe with sharp teeth
Or three eyes on their face.

They could be short or tall
Not have arms and legs at all
They could either walk or slide
Or maybe even crawl.

Can they breathe O_2
Maybe they do
They watch us from afar
What a magnificent view.

How would they react?
Could we have a peaceful pact?
That would be so cool
And I know that for a fact.

Jay Balmer (14)
Ormiston Horizon Academy, Tunstall

Imagine You Never Grow Old

N ever growing old,
E verything to your eyes,
V ertical or horizontal,
E verything to your feet
R ight here, right now.

G rowing old shall never happen,
R iding along those countrysides,
O nly on your own,
W inning this life forever and ever.

O nly one day until this starts,
L iving a luxury life for as long as you want,
D ying will never occur.

Craig Jones (13)
Ormiston Horizon Academy, Tunstall

Only If I Had Infinite Money

I woke up one morning, with millions of messages
So I read through them without hesitation.

I was shocked to see how much money I saw in my account.
So I told my friend and family that I got the money.

So I started buying houses, cars and everything new,
Giving them to people that I don't even know.

One day a homeless man came up to me and asked for some money
So I gave him some so he could buy himself a meal.

Abbie Golinski (12)
Ormiston Horizon Academy, Tunstall

Imagine If You Could Climb Into A TV Set

- **I** magine if you could climb into a TV set
- **M** aybe hop in an episode of the Big Bang Theory
- **A** nd be a part of it, you could come out whenever you wanted
- **G** o into Stranger Things and fight off a demigorgan
- **I** magine a world where you could be a part of anything you wanted
- **N** ever be alone, be a part of all your fantasies, be a vampire
- **E** ven join Monica and Rachel in Central Perk for a coffee.

Amelie Barlow (13)
Ormiston Horizon Academy, Tunstall

Imagine If You Were The Last Human

Imagine if you were the last,
Imagine if you were the past,
Imagine if the unknown was known,
Imagine if monsters were real,
If you imagine, it's real.

Imagine a world of terror,
Imagine hell on earth,
Imagine dragons, fire-breathing dragons,
Imagine if every mythical creature was real,
Just imagine it.

Imagine if the world was yours
And yours alone.
Imagine if you ruled it.

AJ Ball (13)
Ormiston Horizon Academy, Tunstall

The Lottery

T he lottery can make dreams
H olidays every day
E ndless amount of food

L ives have changed thanks to the lottery
O nly the luckiest win
T rying the lottery and winning is very lucky
T rying and winning is a lot of people's dreams
E very competitor who loses feels sad
R olls Royces instead of that old Honda Civic
Y es I've won it.

Connor Flesher (12)
Ormiston Horizon Academy, Tunstall

It All Ends

I magine the world ended tomorrow
T hat everything you had worked for was ruined

A nd you would never see your friends or family again
L ife is all gone
L ike it's all gone in a flash, bang!

E nd isn't far off
N o one will be seen ever again
D on't try and waste the life you have left
S uddenly my life flashed before my eyes.

Isabelle Burrows (11)
Ormiston Horizon Academy, Tunstall

If Only...

If only dreams were real
You could do anything you wanted,
Become rich,
Maybe even drive your car into a ditch
But dreams are made of happiness and fun,
Sometimes nightmares occur,
You can achieve anything
And become the first you,
You can be different,
You can change the world,
You can become an animal,
Maybe a mammal,
It's entirely up to you,
So seriously, be different.

Tom Duffy (14)
Ormiston Horizon Academy, Tunstall

Imagine

Late at night, no sound was made,
Not a bird nor a fly, all echoes decayed...

Not much later, a squeaky voice appeared
All around the house.

Imagine if you would've done something,
When you heard the stairs screech and creak...

Imagine you would've run when you had the chance.
You should've hidden, fought back or done something
But now it's too late.

Oscar Robinson (12)
Ormiston Horizon Academy, Tunstall

Imagine If You Went To Hogwarts

Imagine you're a witch with your twin wizard Dan.
You're asleep in an attic
And startled by your twin Dennis.
You claim a letter and read aloud,
You've heard your thoughts aloud.
"I've been accepted at Hogwarts!"
Now you're in London buying your essential needs,
When you're snatched out of the night
And arrive at Hogwarts with an unexpected fright.

Alyssa Bolderson (12)
Ormiston Horizon Academy, Tunstall

Imagine If We Stopped Walking

Imagine if humans weren't here.
Imagine if we stopped walking the Earth.
Surprisingly that could be a good thing,
But others would disagree.
What if this virus gets too strong and wipes us out
Or if World War Four was fought with sticks and stones
Or if we go back
And the rock didn't wipe the dinosaurs out,
Or would that happen to us?
What would happen without us?

Ben Luis Oliver (13)
Ormiston Horizon Academy, Tunstall

Imagine If Kids Ruled The World

Imagine if we flipped the switch
And kids ruled the world,
Adults just twirled,
Curled into a ball,
As kids stood tall.
Imagine if kids ruled the world,
Kids ran for president,
As adults did the evidence.
Imagine if kids ruled the world,
Adults are babies,
Kids say maybe,
Adults are shady,
Baby, kids, adults,
Imagine if kids ruled the world.

Lottie Hancock (11)
Ormiston Horizon Academy, Tunstall

Imagine If I Was Invisible

Imagine if I was invisible,
I could steal anything from shops without them noticing.
Imagine if I was invisible
I could get lots of people in trouble.
Imagine if I was invisible
I could play pranks on people.

If I was invisible
I would help people by finding their missing items
And putting them back.
If I was invisible
I could be good or bad.

Jacob Fryer (11)
Ormiston Horizon Academy, Tunstall

Dreams

Imagine if your dream came true,
Go to the best places,
Get all the best food.
Imagine if your dream came true,
Life would be cool,
Do whatever you want to do.
Imagine if your dream came true,
Meet all the best people,
See all of the landmarks.
Imagine if your dream came true,
All good technology,
All the best shows.

Eliza Glenn (12)
Ormiston Horizon Academy, Tunstall

Imagine

I f only we were equal, all of us treated the same. No more
M isogyny, homophobia, or hate ever
A gain. Equality for
G ays, women and POC.
I f we could all be ourselves with
N o one being mocked.
E quality for all and acceptance for everyone. Imagine what a wonderful world that would be.

Eleanor Green (13)
Ormiston Horizon Academy, Tunstall

Coronavirus

C are for others
O nly go out if you need to
V isitors not allowed
I t's important to talk to people
D on't break the rules.

So here is to the workers,
The binmen and medical researchers.
I've written the verse
In praise for our nurses
And all keyworkers.

Dale Jenkins-Ferriday (13)
Ormiston Horizon Academy, Tunstall

Imagine If...

I magine if dreams were real
M aybe you could be invisible
A nd kids could rule the world
G oing to the moon
I n an alien spaceship
N o one could say no
E ven if they are all powerful.

I magine if anything was possible
F or that would be amazing.

Ella Potts (13)
Ormiston Horizon Academy, Tunstall

Imagine If They Knew The You, You

Y ou're hiding you know
O ut of the cage and into another
U nder the mask you hide behind

Y ou're not going to be forgiven if they know
O ut of your mind, oh wait, you're trapped in it
U nder that mask no one has seen except your victims at their last scream.

Lily Talbot (12)
Ormiston Horizon Academy, Tunstall

Imagine If The World Was Equal

Imagine if the world was equal,
Earth 2.0 the sequel.
No gender, no race,
What a wonderful place.
What a world this would be.

Imagine no judgement of sexuality,
Finally a place of normality.
No one with more or less,
A recipe for happiness.
What a world this would be.

Daniel Moran (13)
Ormiston Horizon Academy, Tunstall

Imagine If You Could Get Away With Anything

Imagine if you could get away with anything!
You could steal anything.
You could buy a shop or steal it.
You could slap anyone and get away with it.
You could steal a car,
Break someone's back (don't do that though).
You could steal an aeroplane
Or drive anywhere.

Lola Tyler (11)
Ormiston Horizon Academy, Tunstall

Save The Planet

Imagine...
Imagine if you had one wish,
What would it be?
Mine is to win this compeition
Which I'm sure yours is too.
But one wish we all think of...
Is saving the planet.
Act fast!
Act now!
Before we don't have a planet.
Imagine, imagine, imagine.

Sharna Laud (11)
Ormiston Horizon Academy, Tunstall

The TV

There was a TV
In a living room,
It shone like a new penny
But the TV was never on.
In fact the TV was never on
Because nobody used it at all,
In fact the TV was special,
The TV watched you,
Every move you make,
Every breath you take,
It was watching you.

Joseph Moorse (13)
Ormiston Horizon Academy, Tunstall

Space Fights

S tarships
P urging
A lmost every
C elestial system
E ven

F ighting
I n
G hastly space
H ailstorms and
T hrough restricted
S tar systems and dangerous asteroid belts.

Joel Sims (13)
Ormiston Horizon Academy, Tunstall

Imagine

Imagine if I could see how I'm going to die.
I could travel to see how I would look as an adult,
See if the virus ended in 2021.
I would check to see what technology there is.
Imagine you're the only one in the world,
You could win the lottery every time.

Katie Guy (13)
Ormiston Horizon Academy, Tunstall

If I Was Invisible

If I was invisible
I would be the king of the world,
Everything would be my way because I am invisible.
I would get food from the shops
And give the poor food.
I would give the homeless a home.
I would make the unhappy happy
Because I am invisible.

Reuben Dapaah Bonsu
Ormiston Horizon Academy, Tunstall

You Imagine Me

You imagine my hair as white as snow,
With big black boots pounding as I go,
As what is on my back is a massive red sack.

You imagine me to stomp on your roof but don't wake you up,
Then to slide down your chimney and eat a little snack.

Then to walk up your stairs
And see your little cat,
As she meows and meows for a small snack.

Then you imagine me to be pouring out her Dreamies,
As she or he munches away,
And I think to myself,
I must go because I cannot stay.

Then as I see you all tucked in your beds,
I fill your stockings to the very top and run away.
Then you imagine me to run back downstairs
And put your present under the tree.

Then my tiny elves pull me up,
Out of the chimney and put me in the sleigh,
I say goodbye to that last house on the block,
And wish them a Merry Christmas from me!

Sienna Smith (11)
St Mark's West Essex Catholic School, Harlow

Imagine

When boredom hits you during the day
And everything in your mind turns grey,
Imagination is the cure,
Which really works, that's for sure.
Try it yourself and you will see
That this is fun and time consuming, for free...

Imagine a mouse driving a car
And a giraffe playing the guitar.
A submarine flying to space,
With an alien that shows you an undiscovered place.
A flamingo that is blue and green,
Which is the prettiest thing you have ever seen.
Imagine an alien that lives on Mars,
That is scared of sleeping under the stars.
A bird that doesn't have wings,
A sloth that dances and sings.
Imagine a road that can turn and twist,
Imagine that all these things exist.

Lucja Ostrowska (11)
St Mark's West Essex Catholic School, Harlow

Imaginary Friend

My friend is a hungry person
She rolls on marshmallows all day
With her pretty smile and blonde hair
Hour upon hour she eats
Small and colourful
The rumbling, tumbling chocolates
And yum, yum, yum, yum
My friend always laughs
Licking her lips.

And when night wind sleeps
And the moon lay in the sweet clouds
She jumps in joy and sniffing for food
Shaking her sprinkles into a bowl
And sings and hums long and loud
But on quiet nights in May or June
When even the sweet on the dune
Play much more to her tune
With her head in her marshmallows
She lay on fluffy white clouds
So sweet, so sweet, she sweetly sleeps.

Willow Druce (11)
St Mark's West Essex Catholic School, Harlow

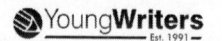

Imagine If You Could See The Future

Imagine if you could see the future,
We would be able to save nature,
We could see if we stopped global warming,
If we didn't that would be a warning.
Would we live in a peaceful world,
Living hand-in-hand, boy and girl,
Would we have put an end to racism?
And also don't forget about sexism.
Would we be able to love who we want
Without being targeted, harassed and much, much more?
Would people accept the PRIDE movement?
Marriage, pregnancy and engagement,
Would we have put an end to abuse
Towards children, animals and adults too?
Imagine if we could see the future,
Wouldn't the world be a lot greater?

Isabel Nye (11)
St Mark's West Essex Catholic School, Harlow

Imagine

Imagine if Coronavirus didn't exist,
Imagine what the world would be,
Not wearing masks everywhere,
Not sanitising every five minutes.
No masks,
No gloves,
But now, no kisses, no hugs,
Imagine if Coronavirus didn't exist.
Without Corona we could see our loved ones,
But now we can't see anyone,
Social distancing - two metres,
Watching funny TikToks and angry Tweeters.
Coronavirus all over the news,
Putting people in the blues,
Boris doing his speech,
The virus out of his reach.
People losing family,
Nan, Dad and your bestie, Amelie,
Imagine if Coronavirus didn't exist.

Evie Wills (11)
St Mark's West Essex Catholic School, Harlow

The Immortal Wheel

The wheel of death and immortal spins,
It kills them,
But they don't die,
The wheel couldn't rest nor sleep,
It kills them all day and all night,
The wheel killed and killed with measured need,
It rose to afflict them, filled with agony and greed.
In women and men's contentment
And overzealous laughter
I called the wheel Samhain,
Now I call it a hideous mosquito.

Karson Dhakal (14)
St Mark's West Essex Catholic School, Harlow

You're In A Computer

You're free to do what you master
You master, you create,
It is like a world of freedom
But you're not in real-life,
But you're cold like ice
And you have a nice design.
The kid is coming so I must hide again,
The next will be the best so let me come again,
Don't turn me off or you're going to feel my pain.

Naglis Arlauskas (11)
St Mark's West Essex Catholic School, Harlow

Imagine

Imagine yourself achieving.
Imagine yourself believing.
Imagine yourself flying high to reach the sky.
Imagine a better world.
Imagine everyone had equal rights.
Imagine getting your dream score.
Imagine having your dream life.
Why do we need to imagine when we can create our world instead?

Christina Lacey (12)
St Mark's West Essex Catholic School, Harlow

The Office

I am getting a job,
One weird one after all,
Cold like ice,
Scared like a slithering snake,
The time has come
To make a change,
To see the agents once again,
I hope I passed but failed again,
Let me pass to my jet,
Because I am the best you will know,
Let me come again.

Jenna Bennett (11)
St Mark's West Essex Catholic School, Harlow

Imagine

Imagine a pig
In a pink wig!
Imagine a star
Shaped as a car!
Imagine a bear
Wearing pink underwear!
Imagine a shoe
Made just for you!
Just imagine.

Kajus Skauronas (11)
St Mark's West Essex Catholic School, Harlow

YoungWriters Est. 1991

YOUNG WRITERS INFORMATION

We hope you have enjoyed reading this book – and that you will continue to in the coming years.

If you're a young writer who enjoys reading and creative writing, or the parent of an enthusiastic poet or story writer, do visit our website www.youngwriters.co.uk. Here you will find free competitions, workshops and games, as well as recommended reads, a poetry glossary and our blog. There's lots to keep budding writers motivated to write!

If you would like to order further copies of this book, or any of our other titles, then please give us a call or order via your online account.

Young Writers
Remus House
Coltsfoot Drive
Peterborough
PE2 9BF
(01733) 890066
info@youngwriters.co.uk

Join in the conversation!
Tips, news, giveaways and much more!

f YoungWritersUK   @YoungWritersCW   @YoungWritersCW